LIBRARY

15
16
17
18
19
20
21
22
ANIMALS
ANIMALS
ANIMALS
ANIMALS
ANIMALS
ANIMALS
ARO PUB
ARO PUB
ARO PUB
ARO PUB
ARO PUB

23
24
25
26
27
28
29
ANIMALS
ANIMALS
ANIMALS
ANIMALS
ANIMALS
ARO PUB
ARY

Snails?

LIBRARY

LIBRAR

Where
do
we
find,

LIBRAR

Whales?

LIBRARY

Where do we find,

Money?

BANK

Where
do
we
find,

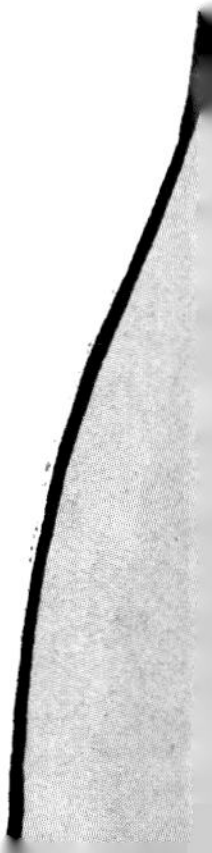

LIBRARY

Honey?

In
books!

In snail books.
In whale books.
In money books.
In honey books.
In books.

LIBRARY